nce upon a time, Don Fambrough, KU's beloved "Coach Fam," was asked to read a story to Janet Stallard's first-grade class at Schwegler Elementary School in Lawrence, Kansas. He was a few sentences into one of his favorites when suddenly he stopped and told the children, "We're going to change it up a little bit."

And so was born "The Three Little Jayhawks" and their adventures with the "big, bad, mean ol' Missouri Tiger." So read on, Jayhawks young and old, and let Coach Fam tell you how it all came to be ...

Second edition, 2007

Publisher: Kevin Corbett, KU Alumni Association
Editor: Jennifer Jackson Sanner
Story Concept: Don Fambrough
Text: Steven Hill, Chris Lazzarino, Susan Younger
Creative Director: Susan Younger
Illustrator: Larry Leroy Pearson

Special thanks to Mike Wellman, Dwight Parman, Valerie Spicher, and Kansas Athletics.
And to our friends at Mizzou, for playing along with good humor.

ISBN 0-9742918-1-1
ISBN 978-0-9742918-1-9

The Three Little Jayhawks

As told by Don Fambrough

Illustrations by Larry Leroy Pearson

ong, long ago atop Mount Oread,
a mother Jayhawk had three little
baby birds. The three little
Jayhawks grew so big
their mother said to them,
"You are too big to live here any longer.
You must go to KU to study and build houses
for yourselves.

"But take care that the big, bad Missouri
Tiger does not catch you."

6   The three little birds set off. "We will take care
that the Tiger does not catch us," they promised.

On Jayhawk Boulevard, they met a man carrying Kansas wheat straw. "Please, will you give me some straw?" asked the first little bird. "I want to build a house for myself."

"Yes," said the man and he gave the first little Jayhawk some straw.

The first little bird built himself a house of straw. He was very content.

"Now the Tiger won't catch me," he said.

8

"I shall build a stronger house than yours," said the second little bird. "Me, too," said the third little bird.

The two little Jayhawks went on along Jayhawk Boulevard. Soon they met a girl carrying sticks she had gathered from the walnut trees in Marvin Grove.

"Please, will you give me some sticks?" asked the second little bird. "I want to build a house for myself."

"Yes," said the girl and she gave the second little bird some sticks.

Then the second little Jayhawk built himself a house of sticks. It was stronger than the house of wheat straw. The second little bird was very pleased. He said, "Now the Tiger won't catch me."

"I shall build a stronger house than yours," said the third little Jayhawk.

The third little bird walked on. Soon he met a man hauling Rock Chalk limestone.

"Please, will you give me some limestone?" asked the third little Jayhawk. "I want to build a house for myself."

"Yes," said the man and he gave the third little bird some stone.

Then the third little Jayhawk built himself a house of Rock Chalk limestone. It took him a long time to build, for it was a very strong house.

The third little Jayhawk was very happy with his house.

"Now the Tiger won't catch me," he said.

13

The next day the big, bad Missouri Tiger came along the boulevard. He came to the house of wheat straw.

When the first little Jayhawk saw the Tiger coming, he ran inside and shut the door.

15

The Tiger scratched on the door and said, "Little bird, little bird, let me in."

"No, no," said the little Jayhawk. "By the feathers of my chinny chin chin, I will not let you in."

"Then I'll huff and I'll puff and I'll blow your house in," said the Tiger.

So he huffed and he puffed and he puffed and he huffed.

Down fell the house of wheat—with wheat waving everywhere in the wind. The little bird was too fast for the Tiger, and he quickly ran to the house of sticks.

16

The Tiger prowled farther along the boulevard. He came to the house of sticks. When the two little birds saw the Tiger coming, they ran inside and shut the door. The Tiger scratched on the door and said, "Little birds, little birds, let me in."

"No, no," said the little Jayhawks. "By the feathers of our chinny chin chins, we will not let you in."

"Then I'll huff and I'll puff and I'll blow your house in," said the Tiger.

So he huffed and he puffed and he puffed and he huffed.

Down fell the house of sticks.

But the two little Jayhawks were too fast for the Tiger, and they quickly ran to the house of Rock Chalk limestone.

The next day the Tiger walked farther along the boulevard. He came to the house of limestone that the third little Jayhawk had built.

When they saw the Tiger coming, all three birds ran inside and shut the door.

The Tiger scratched on the door and said, "Little birds, little birds, let me in."

"No, no," said the little Jayhawks. "By the feathers of our chinny chin chins, we will not let you in."

"Then I'll huff and I'll puff and I'll blow your house in," said the Tiger.

So he huffed and he puffed and he puffed and he huffed. But the house of limestone did not fall down.

The Tiger was very angry, but he pretended not to be. He thought, "This is a clever little bird. If I want to catch him I must pretend to be his friend."

So the Tiger said, "Little bird, be ready at six o'clock in the morning, and I will take you to the Farmer's Market. We shall find some nice bird seed for breakfast."

"Very well," said the little bird.

But the third little bird was a clever little bird. The next morning he set off for the Farmer's Market at five o'clock. He filled his basket with bird seed, then hurried home.

At six o'clock the Tiger knocked on the door. "Are you ready, little bird?" he asked.

"Oh! I have been to the Farmer's Market," said the little bird. "I filled my basket with bird seed and now we are eating breakfast."

The Tiger was very angry, but he pretended not to be. He said, "Be ready at five o'clock in the morning, and I will take you to the pear trees by the Chi-O fountain. We will pick some nice juicy pears."

"Very well," said the little bird.

Next morning, the little bird set off at four o'clock. He found the pear trees. He was up in a tree, picking pears, when the Tiger came along.

24

The little bird was very frightened, but he pretended not to be. He said, "These are fine pears, Mr. Tiger. I'll throw you one." He threw down a pear, and it splashed into the Chi-O fountain. The Tiger, forgetting that cats hate water, jumped in after it, then started crying.

25

26

The little bird jumped down from the tree. He ran all the way home and shut his door quickly.

The Tiger was very angry, but he still pretended not to be.

He went to the little bird's house and knocked on the door. "Little bird," he said, "if you will be ready at four o'clock this afternoon, I will take you to Potter Lake. We will have fun skipping rocks from the bridge."

"Very well," said the little bird.

At two o'clock the little bird set off for
Potter Lake. He had great fun, playing on
the bridge and skipping rocks. Then he found
a big Kansas football by Memorial Stadium.

As the little bird was going home
he saw the Tiger coming up Memorial Drive.
At the right moment, he threw his football
and knocked the Tiger down.

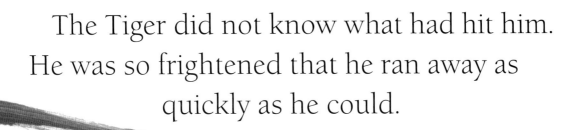

The Tiger did not know what had hit him.
He was so frightened that he ran away as
quickly as he could.

Little Jayhawk
picked up his new football
and he carried it home.

31

The next day the Tiger came and knocked on the little bird's door.

He said, "Little Jayhawk, I did not go to the lake yesterday. A great big thing flew out of nowhere, hit me in the head and knocked me over."

"Ha-ha!" said the little bird. "That was me, with my Kansas football!" The three little Jayhawks laughed so hard they fell on the floor.

When the Tiger heard this, he was very, very angry indeed.

He said, "Little Jayhawks, I am going to climb down your chimney and eat you."

All three little Jayhawks were very frightened, but they said nothing. They put a big pot of water on the fire to boil.

The Tiger climbed on the roof and plunged down the chimney.

The Jayhawks took the lid off the pot. In fell the Tiger, with a big splash.

And that was the end of the big, bad Missouri Tiger.

The clever little Jayhawks enjoyed Tiger soup for months.

The End

"Coach Fam"

Don Fambrough was a freshman at the University of Texas when it came time for him to join his classmates, and other young men from across America, in fighting World War II. While wearing a uniform far different from the football pads he so loved, young Don Fambrough befriended Ray Evans, perhaps the finest all-around athlete and gentleman ever to compete for the University of Kansas.

"Ray was very influential," Fam recalls, "and he talked me into coming here. I never regretted it for one second."

The young man who later would be known by Jayhawks worldwide as "Coach Fam" first established himself as one of KU's best-ever offensive linemen, then went on to a long career as an assistant coach and two stints as head coach.

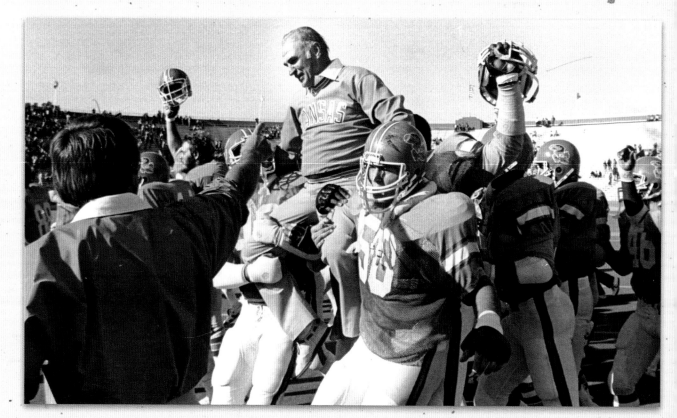

I n retirement, Coach Fam does all he can to perpetuate KU legends, lore and spirit, especially when he delivers his annual address to the football team before the Jayhawks' game against the University of Missouri.

Coach Fam defines a large part of himself by his love for the Crimson and Blue, but he is much more: He earned his University of Kansas degree from the School of Education, and his bride of 60 years, the elegant Del Fambrough, sent forth from Lawrence High School students better versed in the English language,

thanks to her gentle, authoritative guidance and inspiration.

Of course a good coach is first and foremost a good teacher, but Coach Fam says he also could have made a happy life for himself even without the coaching, so long as he had a classroom full of young minds to reach.

"I think if I'd had my choice, I'd probably want that first grade," he says. "They're so eager to learn, so eager to know things. And I know that's a result of good teaching, and good teachers, people who have passion and know how to get to these kids. I know because I was married to one for 60 years."

So it was that Coach Fam eagerly accepted Ms. Janet Stallard's invitation to read to her first-grade class at Schwegler Elementary School, and he beams as he recounts his adventure.

Coach Fam through the years: As a young assistant coach in the 1950s (top left); getting carried off the field after the Jay-hawks' 19-11 triumph over Missouri (left), the victory that sent KU to the 1981 Hall of Fame Bowl in Birmingham, Ala.; outside the KU football locker room (top right); and at Rock Chalk Ball 2005 (above) with (l to r) Edith Darby Evans, widow of his lifelong friend Ray Evans, and Sandy and Mike Wellman.

37

Dear Coach Fambrough,
Thank you for telling
us the story of the
three little jayhawks.
I loved it and your
KU stuff was awasome!
I loved the helmits that
you brought.

Dear Coach. Fam
Thanks for coming
our first grade classr
Thank you for sharit
yourKU things. I hope y
can come again.
Thanks for telling us
The three little jay hawks
and the big bad Missouri
tiger. I loved it!

38

"That was the cutest bunch of kids you ever saw. So cordial, so friendly, so intelligent. I don't know if they got anything out of it, but I sure did!"

While reading "The Three Little Pigs," Coach Fam decided to make a few casting changes. He told the children what he was thinking of doing—in football, changing the play at the last possible second is known as "calling an audible at the line"— and they cried out that he just couldn't!

"No, no, no!" they told their visitor. "That's not the way it goes!"

So Coach Fam explained some more, and told the children about KU's long rivalry with the University of Missouri, whose mascot, the Tiger, would take the place of the Big Bad Wolf.

"And oh boy, they got right in the middle of that!" Fam remembers. "You could tell, even the first graders, they'd heard about our rivalry with Missouri! So they loved this story."

When the story was done, the girls took their new friend by the hand and led him outside for recess. On the playground, they taught him how to play hopscotch, and old Coach Fam was young again.

Sharing KU Spirit: Coach Fam during his improvised reading of "The Three Little Jayhawks" to Janet Stallard's first-grade class at Schwegler Elementary School (left); excerpts from the children's thank-you letters (below), which are now among Fam's most cherished possessions; and sharing a laugh with fellow Jayhawk football legend Gale Sayers at a reception at The Outlook, the Chancellor's residence on Lilac Lane.

Dear Coach Fambrough,
I really enjoyed the things you showed me. I uptesheate the things you showed me. The best part was your story. I liked your imaghashin.

Dear Coach Fambrough,
I liked the story about The little Jayhawks and the mean bad Missouri tiger.
That story was great! I thought that was he best story I ever heard!

39

About the Artist

Larry Leroy Pearson has been a contributing artist to *Kansas Alumni* magazine for more than two decades. An Oklahoma native and OU grad, Pearson fell in love with Mount Oread after moving to Lawrence in the '80s. His delightful depictions of the Jayhawk have become one of the magazine's favorite traditions. *The Three Little Jayhawks* is a children's book created exclusively for the KU Alumni Association.

Photo Credits: p. 36, Spencer Research Library (2); p. 37, Earl Richardson, Spencer Research Library; p. 38, Janet Stallard; p. 39, Earl Richardson